Casey Little
Yo-Yo Queen

NANCY BELGUE

ORCA BOOK PUBLISHERS

National Library of Canada Cataloguing in Publication Data

Belgue, Nancy, 1951-
Casey Little yo-yo queen / Nancy Belgue.

(Orca young readers)
ISBN 1-55143-357-5

I. Title. II. Series.

PS8553.E4427C37 2005   jC813'.6   C2005-905191-4

First published in the United States, 2005
Library of Congress Control Number: 2005932257

Summary: When a magical carnival sets up across the street from Casey Little's house, it turns out that she will have to overcome her deepest fear if she is to have any chance of making her dream come true.

Free teachers' guide available at www.orcabook.com

Orca Book Publishers gratefully acknowledges the support for its publishing programs provided by the following agencies: the Government of Canada through the Book Publishing Industry Development Program (BPIDP), the Canada Council for the Arts, and the British Columbia Arts Council.

Typesetting and cover design by Lynn O'Rourke
Cover & interior illustrations by Samia Drisdelle

In Canada:
Orca Book Publishers
Box 5626 Stn. B
Victoria, BC Canada
V8R 6S4

In the United States:
Orca Book Publishers
PO Box 468
Custer, WA USA
98240-0468

www.orcabook.com
Printed and bound in Canada.
08 07 06 05 • 6 5 4 3 2 1

To John and Daniel,
who make every day magical!

# CHAPTER 1

"You won't believe what I just saw!" Casey Little whispered to her best friend, Mickey.

Mickey slouched down under his spy hat and went on dusting his kitchen table for fingerprints. He grunted.

"Stop fooling around, Mickey," Casey said, nudging him with her elbow. "Come here and look!"

"I'm not fooling around," Mickey said, looking up from his notepad. "I'm finding out who ate the last donut." He pointed to the plate, sprinkled with chocolate crumbs and fingerprint dust. "I was saving that donut for lunch!"

"Forget the donut. The new neighbor just had a pinball machine delivered to her house."

"Sure. And I just did a Nollie 360 kick-flip."

"No, really. The delivery men are just leaving."

Casey pulled Mickey's sleeve. He came over to the window. A big truck was pulling away from the house across the street. *Phil's Vending Machines* was written in bright red letters on its side.

Across the street, Mrs. Lombardi's house sat smugly in the sun. The curtains were drawn.

As Casey and Mickey watched, the lawn sprinklers spurted to life, filling the yard with tiny rainbows.

"What would an old lady like that want with a pinball machine?" Casey asked.

Mickey shrugged. "We could spy on her and find out."

Casey shook her head. "Maybe she's trying to attract kids into her house so she can eat them!"

Mickey smiled. "I don't think so. I heard my mom tell my dad that Mrs. Lombardi's a vegetarian."

"Your mom talked to her?" Casey turned to Mickey, her eyes wide. "I didn't think anyone had ever seen her."

"Sure. My mom knocked on her door the day she moved in." Mickey had gone back to studying the empty plate. "I think my brother, Felix, ate the donut," he said at last.

"Are those his fingerprints?" Casey asked, peering at the plate and forgetting Mrs. Lombardi for a minute.

Mickey shook his head and pointed out the back window. Felix was pedaling his tricycle up and down the driveway. Chocolate was smeared from one end of his mouth to the other.

"Good detective work, Mickey," Casey said.

"There's more than one kind of evidence, you know," Mickey said indignantly. "Sometimes all the proof you need is right in front of your eyes."

Mickey's mother poked her head in the back door. "I'm taking Felix to the park. Do you want to come?" Mickey folded up his fingerprint kit and nodded.

"What about you, Casey?" asked Mrs. Mitchell.

Casey shook her head. "I've got work to do."

Mrs. Mitchell smiled. "How many have you got on your list this week, Casey?"

"Three," Casey said proudly. "Mrs. Richardson's dog, the Singhs' fish and the Littlejohns' snakes."

"How's your horse fund coming along?"

"I have three hundred dollars saved already. Only one thousand two hundred dollars to go!" Casey was saving all her money to buy Lightning, her favorite horse. The riding stable where Casey rode was being sold because the owner was retiring. Casey had worked really hard all summer to save three hundred dollars.

"That's amazing. Well, come on then,

boys." Mrs. Mitchell bustled around the kitchen, throwing snacks into a canvas sack.

"Notice anything missing?" Mickey asked his mother, staring at the empty plate.

Mrs. Mitchell patted Mickey on the head. "No, dear."

"The donut?"

Mrs. Mitchell smiled. "Did Felix get it?"

"It's not funny, Mom."

Casey could still hear Mickey complaining as he followed his mother and brother down the street. She stood for a minute, then checked her pocket for the keys. She had each family's key on a separate ring, labeled with their name. She would start with the Singh house. Casey fished out the Singhs' house key and crossed the street, still staring at Mrs. Lombardi's.

She let herself in the back door, just the way Mrs. Singh had showed her. Casey had started her pet-sitting business in the spring. At first her mom had thought that ten was too young to take on so much responsibility. But so many people had called after she'd delivered the flyer she'd printed up on her computer that her mom had let her take customers as long as they lived on her street.

Casey liked the Singhs' house. Pictures of foreign buildings with pointed roofs hung all over the walls, and the furniture was bright and inviting. A gigantic aquarium stood in the opening between the kitchen and the dining room.

Some of the brightly colored fish floated lazily in the deep green water, while others flashed by like little neon signs. Casey sprinkled fish food into the tank, watered the ficus tree in the living room and brought in the flyers that someone had tossed on the lawn. Then she let herself out the back door, making sure she locked it behind her.

That done, she took another key out of her pocket. The snakes were next. When her customers came home from their vacations, she would have another fifty dollars for her horse fund. She was just thinking how long it would be before she would be able to buy Lightning, when the curtain flickered in Mrs. Lombardi's living-room window.

A shiver ran down Casey's spine, and the story of Hansel and Gretel popped into her head. She looked around nervously for breadcrumbs. Why did Mrs. Lombardi give her the shivers? The little stone house looked innocent enough. It was just that no one had ever seen Mrs. Lombardi, Casey decided. At least none of the kids on Willow Street had ever seen her.

"Casey!" Brenda Bristowe shouted from her swing. "Come here!"

Casey trotted over to Brenda's fence.

"Did you hear about Zelda?" Brenda said.

Casey shook her head. Zelda owned the stable where Casey and Brenda rode. Casey glanced back over her shoulder.

There! She'd seen it again: a flicker of lace in the window. That old lady was watching her!

"Well," Brenda went on as she pumped her legs, starting the swing moving, "she fell off Blister at the horse show on Sunday and broke her leg. My mom said she's going to have to sell the stable even sooner than she thought and that Lightning's sure to be the first to go."

Casey's head snapped back toward Brenda. Brenda was pumping harder now, and her pigtails floated in the air behind her.

"What did you say?" Casey shouted.

"I said," Brenda shouted back, "Zelda's selling Lightning!"

"No!" Casey cried, taking a step back. "I don't believe you!"

Brenda dragged her heels, slowing the swing.

"It's the truth. You can ask my mom." Brenda stuck her upturned nose even farther into the sky. "Guess you won't be able to buy him after all."

"I will." Casey reached over and yanked one of Brenda's pigtails. "Just you see if I don't!"

Brenda's eyes widened. "You attacked me!" she screeched. "You tried to pull my hair out!"

Casey hardly heard her. She was running as fast as she could toward her house.

"Mom!" she yelled as she slammed through the front door.

Her mother was just hanging up the phone. She had a worried look on her face.

"Who was that?" Casey asked, pointing at the phone, feeling the tears prickle at the back of her eyes.

"I guess you know," her mother said, looking at her face. She came toward Casey. "I'm sorry, sweetheart. Zelda wanted to tell you herself, but you weren't home. She was hoping to give you the news before you heard it from someone else." Casey's mom glanced out the window toward Brenda's house.

"But Mom, I have three hundred dollars. Can't she wait?"

"I know how much Lightning means to you, honey, but Zelda has to pay her bills. Someone has offered her fifteen hundred dollars cash for him. She can't wait anymore. She needs the money."

"It's not fair!" Casey sobbed. She ran to her room and slammed the door.

Lightning couldn't be sold. He couldn't! After what had happened at the school talent show last spring, Lightning was practically her only friend. Brenda and her gang teased her all the time about that awful day. The only place she ever felt really happy was when she was up on Lightning's back. Then she believed she could do anything and could almost forget what a fool she'd made of herself. She had to save Lightning!

But where was she going to get twelve hundred dollars in time?

CHAPTER 2

Casey stared at the snakes in their terrariums: two corn snakes and a ball python. She turned on their lights and their heating pads and refilled their dishes with fresh water. She replaced the wire-mesh lids on their cages and weighted them down with large rocks. The orange corn snake slithered up the side of the glass and tried to poke its nose through the mesh. Casey watched it, feeling just as trapped. She was never going to save enough money in time to buy Lightning.

She sighed and went to water Mrs. Littlejohn's African violets that were sunning themselves on the front windowsill. That's when she saw it. Casey's eyes goggled. Another truck had pulled into Mrs. Lombardi's driveway. Two men were unloading a candy-floss machine.

Casey watched the driver and his helper put the machine onto a dolly and wheel it up the driveway, around the corner and into Mrs. Lombardi's backyard. Casey only realized she was craning her neck when she poured water all over her foot.

"Eeek," she squealed and looked down at the puddle on the wooden floor. She dashed out to the kitchen and grabbed a towel from the rack. First a pinball machine, now a machine to make cotton candy. What was going on?

Casey rubbed the spot dry and hung the towel back on the rack. She pinched a few dead blossoms off the African violets, just the way Mrs. Littlejohn had shown her, but her mind was not on her work. It was on all the strange things that were happening in the little stone house across the road.

As she was locking the door, she spied Mickey, Felix and Mrs. Mitchell coming back from the park. She ran down the sidewalk to meet them.

"Mickey," she said, after Felix and Mrs. Mitchell had gone back inside, "you'll never guess what I saw now."

Mickey stared glumly at the apple his mother had given him. "No," he said. He looked at Casey. "How can any mother think an apple is just as good as a chocolate-covered donut?"

"Mickey, forget the donut for a minute. I need you to help me solve another mystery."

"Should I give in and eat it?" he asked, turning the apple over in his hands.

"Mickey!" Casey shouted.

"Oh, all right!" Mickey put the apple on the steps. He turned and looked Casey right in the eye. "What's up?"

"A cotton-candy machine, that's what's up!" Casey said. She pointed at Mrs. Lombardi's house. "I saw one delivered while you were at the park."

"No kidding?" Mickey stared at the house across the street. "I love cotton candy."

"I know!" Casey yelled. "But what do you think an old lady like that wants with a cotton-candy machine and a pinball machine?"

"Hmmmmm," Mickey said. He narrowed his eyes and rubbed his chin. He always did that when he was detecting something. Casey sat still and waited.

"Hmmmm," Mickey said again. "I don't really know," he admitted.

"Oh." Casey was disappointed. Mickey always had an answer. They sat and stared at the stone house.

"Let's go over and spy on her," Mickey suggested.

"Well, maybe we could just peek around back of the house," Casey said.

They stood up. The street seemed as wide as an ocean. A cool breeze ruffled Casey's hair. She shivered. The flesh prickled along her arms. Even Mickey wasn't walking as fast as he usually did.

"What if she's getting all this stuff so she can trick kids like us into her back-yard so she can turn us into statues or something?" Casey whispered as they reached the bottom of the driveway. The driveway was paved with bricks, and grass was poking up through the cracks. A shiny black crow cawed from a wire overhead.

Mickey stopped. Casey heard him gulp. She glanced over. He was staring at the front window. "I thought I saw something." His voice shook.

Casey inched closer to Mickey's side and took his hand. She looked at the window, but all she could see was the sun glinting off the glass. The two friends hesitated. Should they go up the driveway or not?

"Casey!" Mom hollered as she opened the front door. "If you want to get to your riding lesson on time, we've got to go! Have you finished your pet-sitting visits?"

"Not yet!" Casey hollered back.

"Well, hurry up! We're leaving in ten minutes."

16

Mickey heaved a sigh of relief; Casey was sure of it.

He wiped his palm on his jacket and took another look at the house. "I saw a face looking out the front window. I know I did!"

"Let's come back later and check it out," Casey said.

"Okay."

They crossed the street again, neither one looking back, but Casey was sure she could feel eyes watching her all the way home.

She could still feel those eyes on her when she turned over the rock where the Richardsons hid their door key. They were the only family that didn't give Casey her own set of keys when they went away. From inside the house she could hear Benny, the black Lab, barking in excitement. Benny loved going for his walk. Casey went around to the back and opened the door. Benny barreled out of the house as if he'd been shot from a cannon. He rolled, jumped up and ran toward Casey at full speed. She braced herself as he flung himself against her legs and licked her hands.

In spite of her sadness about Lightning and her lingering fear about the strange house, Casey couldn't help but laugh. Benny always cheered her up.

Casey ran around the Richardsons' fenced-in backyard while Benny chased her. Finally he stopped to smell the rabbits that lived under the hedge that bordered the back of the yard, and Casey flopped down on the grass. It was the end of August, and the day was bright and sunny. Big white clouds sailed through a deep blue sky. Casey tried to see shapes. She made out a giant rabbit with ears as big as a house. "Benny wouldn't dare chase *you*," she said out loud.

At the sound of his name, Benny charged over and dropped a ball on her stomach. Casey sat up and tossed it into the back of the yard. Benny took off like he'd been catapulted out of a slingshot. Casey lay back down.

A dragon cloud floated by. And a tulip. Casey tossed Benny's ball again, and he raced across the yard as if he'd never chased a ball before in his life. Casey watched him snuffling around under the big fir tree, pawing at his ball, which had rolled under its lowest branches. The bird chorus kept time with his waving tail. Casey lay back and squinted at the sky. She watched a cloud change shape from a sailboat to a flying goose to a...horse.

All the sadness came back.

Lightning was going to be sold. Today might be her last chance to ride him.

Casey sat up and whistled for Benny. He nuzzled her palm, looking for pats. Casey rubbed his ears and wiped off his paws and put him in the house. "I'll see you later, boy," she told him when he looked at her with his sad brown eyes. His baton of a tail hung motionless between his legs.

"You look like I feel," Casey told him. He whined and dropped his head onto his paws.

Mom was waiting in the car when Casey got home.

"You know, Casey, if you are going to take on the responsibility of a job, you have to learn to manage your time better. You're going to be late for your lesson."

"What does it matter anyway?" Casey muttered as she pulled on the riding boots her mother had put on the back seat.

Mom didn't answer. She was looking out the back window as she reversed down the driveway with one hand hooked over the seat back and one hand on the steering wheel.

She guided the car onto the road and turned toward Main Street.

"What do you mean, what does it matter?" Mom asked as they turned the corner.

"I thought you didn't hear me," Casey said.

"I heard you. I know you're disappointed about Lightning, Casey. But owning a horse costs a lot of money, and

I don't think we can afford it. Even if you managed to save up enough to buy him, we would still have to pay to board him and feed him. You have to be realistic."

Casey stared at her mom. "Why did you let me think I could buy him?"

Mom looked over and sighed. "I didn't think Zelda would have to make a decision so quickly. I was waiting for the right moment to say something."

Casey couldn't stop the tears from dripping down her face.

Why was it that on some days, nothing ever went right?

CHAPTER 3

Lightning was in the paddock when Casey jumped out of the car. He trotted over and nuzzled her palm. Casey pulled out the apple she had hidden in her pocket and smelled the sweet scent of apple juice as he crunched it between his big yellow teeth.

"Beeeebopalua, that's my baybeeeeee," came the sound of off-key singing from inside the barn. "Beeeeeeeeebopalua, I don't mean maaaaaayyyyybeeeee." Casey followed the twangy voice until she came to the last stall. She poked her head inside. A tall man was sitting on a bale of hay, whittling a small block of wood.

"Who are you?" she asked. The man's legs were stretched out and crossed at the ankles. He looked like a marionette. Casey had never seen him before.

"Well, howdy, young lady," the man said, doffing an imaginary hat. "Allow me to introduce myself. My name, since you ask, is Geronimo Patchett." He kept whittling. Curled shavings dropped at his feet in little piles. The air smelled piney and horsey and strawy.

Casey leaned against the doorframe. She crossed her arms.

"And who, may I ask, are you?" Geronimo said as he held his little carving up for inspection.

"Casey Little," Casey answered.

"Ohhhh," Geronimo said. He gave Casey a careful inspection. "I thought that's who you might be."

Casey took a closer look at the carving. "That's a yo-yo," she said.

"That's right, Miss Casey," Geronimo said. He watched her steadily.

Casey looked him in the eyes. "Are you

the one who wants to buy my horse?" she asked.

"Yup." Geronimo folded his long legs under him and stood up. He seemed to reach the ceiling. "I understand you're pretty fond of that horse."

Casey squinted into the dusty air. She nodded.

"Well, Miss Casey, I can assure you I'll take good care of him."

"Casey!" yelled Zelda from the front of the barn. "You in here?"

"She's right here, Miss Zelda," called Geronimo.

Casey turned and ran for the front of the barn. She whizzed past Zelda and into the paddock. Lightning was waiting at the fence, his ears pricked forward. Casey buried her face in his mane. He nudged her pockets, looking for more apples.

Zelda placed a hand on Casey's shoulder. "I see you met Geronimo," she said.

Casey shook Zelda's hand away. Zelda balanced on her crutches, grabbed Casey's arm and turned her around. "I was hoping to talk to you first, Casey," Zelda said. "I have to sell Lightning because I need the money."

Casey sniffed.

"But Geronimo doesn't live too far away. I think you can still visit Lightning from time to time."

Casey sniffed again and ran her hand over her nose. Zelda handed her a tissue. Casey blew.

Zelda nodded and patted Casey on the arm. Lightning put his head over Casey's shoulder and blew apple-juice breath on her cheek.

Geronimo came to the fence. "Let's see how you ride him, Miss Casey," he said. His eyes had crinkles in the corners and were the color of chocolate cake. His hair stuck straight out from his head in ten different directions, and around his neck he wore a string tie fastened with a tiny silver yo-yo.

"Go on, Casey," Zelda said.

Casey saddled Lightning, swung onto his back and trotted into the paddock.

She guided him over one of the smallest jumps. It didn't matter that Geronimo and Zelda were trying to be nice. Casey knew she was never going to see Lightning after he was sold. Things just didn't work out that way. Oh, sure, Mom would say that they'd go visit, but then she'd never find the time.

Casey tried to enjoy herself, but she didn't have much fun.

On the drive home, she didn't say a word.

When they pulled into the driveway, Mickey was sitting on his front steps, waiting. Casey could tell that he was excited about something by the way he jumped up when he saw them. "Can I go play with Mickey?" she asked.

"All right," Mom said, checking her watch. "But be home in an hour. You have some chores to do."

Mickey was beckoning wildly as Casey ran across the lawn.

"You'll never guess what's happened now!" he said.

"What?"

"Fireworks!"

"Fireworks?"

Mickey pointed at the stone house. "This afternoon. A fireworks delivery truck dropped off a big load at Mrs. Lombardi's."

Casey and Mickey stared at each other. "Pinball machine, cotton-candy machine, fireworks," they said together.

"Punch buggy, no returns," Mickey said. He poked Casey in the arm.

Casey didn't notice. "The curtains twitched again," she said.

A cloud sailed past the sun.

"What do you think is going on?"

"I don't know, but I am going around back," Casey answered.

Mickey followed reluctantly. "I don't know if this is a good idea," he said.

Casey flattened herself against the side of the house. "Shhh!" she said. She beckoned to Mickey.

He crept forward.

"Look!" Casey said.

Mickey craned his neck around Casey's shoulder and stared.

A big striped tent filled Mrs. Lombardi's backyard.

Casey and Mickey stared so hard at the tent they didn't even hear the footsteps.

A shadow snaked over them and onto the grass.

"Hello, children," said a mysterious voice.

Mickey jumped. Casey twirled around.

An old, old, old lady stood looking at them. She was wearing overalls and work boots. Her hair was tied into a wispy white ponytail, and her face looked like a piece of cracked china.

"I'm Mavis Lombardi," the woman said. She held out a wrinkled claw.

Casey and Mickey stared. Casey could feel Mickey's arm twitching beside her. His arm always twitched when he was about to make a break for it.

She grabbed Mickey's hand and held on tight. She tried a tiny smile and hoped she looked normal.

Her hand started to twitch too.

Mrs. Lombardi smiled. "What do you think of the carnival?"

"Carnival?" Casey and Mickey said in one voice. Their hands twitched again.

"You can stop twitching," Mrs. Lombardi said. "I won't hurt you."

Mickey gulped and pulled his hand loose from Casey's. He stuck it in his pocket, where it jiggled up and down. "I'm not twitching," he said.

"Come on, come on," Mrs. Lombardi commanded. "Don't just stand there. You might as well make yourselves useful."

"What do you mean, useful?" Casey asked. She trotted behind Mrs. Lombardi, who was walking very fast considering her age.

Mrs. Lombardi's words floated back over her shoulder. "I'm having a carnival here this weekend," she said. "To introduce myself to the neighborhood."

Behind her, Mickey whispered, "Do you see any brick ovens?"

"Shhhh!" Casey said.

Mrs. Lombardi bustled over to the pinball machine. "I heard that, young man. Don't think I didn't." She gave Mickey a shrewd look. "You afraid of me?"

Mickey shook his head. Mrs. Lombardi glanced at the hand he had stuffed in his pocket. Mickey clamped his other hand over it. Mrs. Lombardi smiled.

She fed a coin to the pinball machine and started banging away on the buttons on the side. Lights flashed, bells clanged, levers flicked up and down. A little silver ball ricocheted around the machine, banging, bopping, clanging, setting off whistles and lights and giving rise to great shouts of excitement from Mrs. Lombardi.

"Get in there, you silver devil!" she yelled.

"No you don't," she hollered as she slapped the machine on the side.

"Gotcha!" she crowed. She flipped the lever and spun the little ball back up to the top of the machine, where it set off another series of bells and whistles.

"All riiiiiight!" she chortled. She danced a little jig, and her white ponytail bounced around the top of her head like a piece of dandelion fluff on a stiff breeze.

"Here, you!" She nodded at Casey. "You look like you've got nerves of steel. Take over!" She flicked the lever one last time and stood aside.

Reluctantly, Casey stepped up to the plate.

"Put your body into it," Mrs. Lombardi instructed.

Casey caught the edge of the little ball just as it rolled past the lever. It wobbled into a hole and was ejected. It careened crazily across the machine like a boxer in the ring, hit the ropes and launched itself straight down the middle.

"Use your body!" Mrs. Lombardi yelled.

Casey didn't know what she meant. She stared at the silver ball as it rolled right past her flipping flippers and into the gutter.

"Never mind," said Mrs. Lombardi. "Next time give the old machine a slap."

She hit the machine's side, and all the lights went out.

"Can I try?" Mickey asked.

Mrs. Lombardi turned and put her hands on her hips.

"Well, you don't say," she said. "No more twitches."

Mickey blushed.

"Come on, kids," Mrs. Lombardi continued. "I always like to finish off a thrilling game of pinball with some cotton candy."

Casey and Mickey followed Mrs. Lombardi over to the cotton-candy machine. She turned it on and poured some sugar into a hole in the middle. The machine whirred around and around and around. The smell of warm sugar wafted into the air, and pink strands of spun sugar appeared inside the machine. Mrs. Lombardi grabbed a paper cone from a stack on a table and twisted the floating shreds of pink floss around the cone. The floss got bigger and bigger until it was the size of a giant beehive.

"Just say when," cackled Mrs. Lombardi.

"When!" Casey and Mickey shouted together.

Mrs. Lombardi handed the giant candy floss to Mickey. "Here you go. This ought to make up for that missing donut!"

"How did you know about that?" asked Mickey. His mouth was beaded with droplets of melted candy floss.

"Overheard you yelling at your mother," Mrs. Lombardi said. She twisted off another giant cone of candy floss and handed it to Casey. "Shouldn't ever yell at your mother," she said sternly. But her eyes twinkled.

"Now, Casey," she said. Casey pulled a piece of candy floss off her stick and fed it into her mouth a little at a time. She stopped. The candy floss melted on her tongue.

"Now, Casey," Mrs. Lombardi repeated. "What are we going to do about you and your horse?"

Casey and Mickey stared at each other.

Mrs. Lombardi didn't seem to notice. She was too busy making the biggest candy floss they'd ever seen. It was the size of a rain barrel. Mrs. Lombardi was invisible behind the pink cloud.

How did she know these things?

Maybe she was a witch after all!

CHAPTER 4

"How did you know about my horse?" Casey asked. Mrs. Lombardi peeked out from behind her cotton candy.

"Got ears, don't I?" she said. A long strand of pink candy floss was attached to her ponytail. It floated out behind her like a banner.

Casey stared at the old lady's ears. They looked like normal ears, not extra-special supersensitive hearing machines.

"Well, kids!" Mrs. Lombardi said. "Friday's the big day. Tell all your friends. This weekend we're having a carnival!" She swooped off into the house with a wave of her candy floss.

Casey and Mickey went back down the walk.

"I still think it's some kind of trick!" Mickey said.

"How did she know those things about us?" Casey wondered. "Is this really happening?"

But the cotton candy was still on their sticks, and they could hear the flapping of the striped tent as it snapped in the breeze. The carnival started on Friday. Only three days away. Would anyone come?

Mickey chewed thoughtfully on his candy floss. "Let's go tell my mother," he said. "See what she thinks." They started toward Mickey's house.

Brenda Bristowe called from her front porch as they crossed the street. "Did you see all that stuff?"

"Yeah!" Mickey shouted. Casey crossed her arms and turned her back. She wasn't ready to be friendly to Brenda yet.

"I'm going to the carnival," Brenda boasted. "Mrs. Lombardi asked me to run the cotton-candy machine, and I said yes!"

Mickey glanced in Casey's direction. Casey's shoulders stiffened.

"Hear that?" he whispered out of the side of his mouth. Casey grunted.

"She didn't give us jobs," Mickey pointed out.

"Maybe she doesn't trust you," Brenda jeered. She had left the porch and was leaning over her fence.

"She does too, Brenda Bristowe," Casey said. She turned around and looked at Brenda through narrowed eyes. "She's saving our jobs for Friday!"

"Oh, sure," Brenda said. "That's a good one!" She barked a fake laugh in their direction and skipped back up her walk.

"What'd you say that for?" Mickey asked. "She didn't say anything about giving us a job."

"I know, I know," Casey muttered. Sometimes that Brenda Bristowe could be just so annoying!

Mickey's mom came to the door and

hollered that dinner would be ready in five minutes. Casey waved good-bye and went to let Benny out for his afternoon walk. Afterward she sat and stared at the stone house. Just who was Mrs. Lombardi anyway?

Mom was setting the table when Casey let herself in the back door.

"All finished with your pet-sitting?" Mom asked.

Casey nodded and grabbed a piece of carrot from the salad. "Mom," she began.

"Yes?" Mom asked. She looked up from the table.

"Have you ever met Mrs. Lombardi?"

"Sure have," Mom said.

"How come you never said anything?"

"Never thought to mention it. But isn't it nice she's having that carnival for the neighbors?"

So Mom knew about the carnival. Casey munched on her carrot. Another truck rolled up to the house, and Casey peered out the window.

Mom came up behind her. "What's she having delivered now?"

The men hopped out of the truck and unloaded a big neon sign.

"My goodness," said Mom.

The men carted the sign onto the front lawn and ran an extension cord up around the side of the house. The sign flashed.

"Goodness gracious," said Mom.

A flashing neon yo-yo blinked off and on. The letters on the sign lit up in bright pink and green.

YO-YO CONTEST

First Prize $1500.00

Casey turned and stared at her mother. "A yo-yo contest?"

Mom's eyes sparkled. "Do you suppose she heard about you?"

"She seems to know everything else," Casey said.

"But Casey, you haven't practiced your yo-yo tricks for months. Mrs. Lombardi only just moved in two weeks ago."

The doorbell jangled through the house. Mickey hammered on the door.

"I'm coming!" Casey shouted.

Mickey pulled Casey onto the porch.

He pointed at the sign. A flashing yo-yo curled and uncurled over the sign's edge.

"Fifteen hundred dollars" was all Mickey could say. "Fifteen hundred dollars," he repeated.

Brenda Bristowe waved at them from her front yard and stuck out her tongue when she got their attention. *No way*, she mouthed at Casey. *You are too chicken!* Then she started clucking and flapping her arms as she strutted around her yard. Casey scowled at her, then turned away.

She flexed and unflexed her fingers.

How could she have known?

How could Mrs. Lombardi have known?

Casey Little was the uncrowned yo-yo queen of Essex County.

"It's a mystery," muttered Mickey as if he'd read her mind.

Across the street, a lace curtain fluttered in the late-August twilight.

# CHAPTER 5

The yo-yo sign on Mrs. Lombardi's front lawn flashed all through dinner.

"That thing's going to drive me nuts," said Casey's dad.

"It's hypnotic," said Mom.

"That sure is a lot of money," Casey said. She forked up a lettuce leaf and popped it into her mouth.

"Once word gets around, she'll have people coming from all over the province," Dad said. "Pass the rolls, please."

Casey chewed thoughtfully. Silence fell upon the room. The only noise was the clinking of the knives and forks on the plates.

Finally Mom said, "I wonder where she comes from. It's kind of unusual for someone to host such a big party."

Dad shook his head. "I've wondered about that myself."

"I think she's a witch," Casey muttered.

"A witch?" Mom laughed. "She may be a bit eccentric. But there really aren't any witches."

"Sure there are," Casey said. "I saw books in the library all about spells and stuff like that."

"Well, people believe in all kinds of things," Dad said. "But as far as I know, witches only exist in fairy tales."

We'll just see about that, Casey decided. After supper she phoned Mickey. They talked while sitting in their kitchen windows so they could see each other.

"Let's go to the library tomorrow," Casey said.

"Why?" Mickey asked. He sounded like he was eating something.

"I want to check on some books about witches. What are you eating, anyway?"

Mickey held up something round. A donut! "Dad brought home a whole box just for me!" he said into the phone.

"Did your mom tell him you wanted one?"

"Nope!" In his kitchen window on the other side of the driveway, Mickey shook his head. "Said the idea just popped into his head while he was driving home from work. Isn't that weird?"

"Weird," Casey muttered. "Hey, Mickey," she started, then stopped.

"Yeah?" Mickey said around a mouthful of donut.

"Oh, nothing."

"Can't stop now," Mickey said.

"It's just." Casey stopped again.

Mickey sighed so loudly that Casey could practically hear him without the phone.

"It's just," Casey rushed on. "It's just that a lot of weird things have been happening since Mrs. Lombardi moved in."

Mickey put down his donut. Both friends turned to stare at the little stone house.

The striped tent seemed to send up a glow from the backyard, surrounding the house with a halo of bright light. Suddenly the flashing neon sign went out.

"Wow," Casey said.

"Yeah," Mickey echoed. "Wow."

For hours Casey lay in bed with her eyes open. She heard Mom and Dad come up the stairs and turn out the downstairs light. She heard the bathroom sounds as Dad brushed his teeth, and the night sounds as Mom padded into Casey's room and opened the window a crack. Casey squished her eyes closed and pretended to be asleep. Mom dropped a kiss on her forehead.

The house was silent and still, but Casey couldn't sleep.

She tossed.

She turned.

She rolled to one side. Then the other.

She felt like a pinball in Mrs. Lombardi's machine.

Finally Casey got up. Something was calling her, keeping her awake. It was something in the closet under a pile of summer clothes.

It was her super-cool, limited-edition, cherry-red yo-yo.

She could practically see it, right through the closet door, glowing in the dark. She opened the door a crack and stared at the place where she'd hidden it. She imagined it lying there, teasing her. Her fingers itched to pick it up. She could feel the cool smoothness of its red lacquer paint. Her hand twitched as she felt the vibrations of the sleeping yo-yo travel up her arm. She closed her eyes and imagined holding on until the very last millisecond before gently but crisply jerking her finger and commanding the yo-yo upward into her waiting palm.

Her eyes flew open.

What was she thinking?

That yo-yo was the cause of the worst moment in her whole entire life.

Stage fright!

That yo-yo was the reason everyone in Harmony Beach laughed at her, the reason

Brenda Bristowe and all her friends said she should change her name from Casey Little to Chicken Little! She had thought she'd never be able to show her face in public again after that terrible, awful, humiliating, embarrassing, curl-up-and-wish-you-were-invisible moment.

Casey slammed the closet door and backed away.

After the school assembly where she'd frozen solid in front of all her friends, she'd vowed never again. Never again would she pick up a yo-yo and perform a trick in front of anyone.

Casey swallowed. Her mouth was full of cotton.

She didn't even know why she'd saved that darn yo-yo. Tomorrow she would throw it out.

That's what she'd do.

She took a deep breath and lay on her bed.

But she couldn't sleep.

That terrible yo-yo memory would not let go.

It followed her around no matter what she tried to think about.

She was up on the stage. The gym was full of whispering, jostling, smiling children. Everyone was looking at her.

"Introducing Casey Little, Yo-Yo Queen," said the principal. A hush fell over the gym. All the faces stared at Casey. Twelve hundred eyes. Six hundred open mouths. Casey froze. The yo-yo felt like a chunk of unformed clay. Her knees wham-bammed against each other. The principal nudged her. She forgot to breathe. The audience squirmed. The principal *harrrumpphed* loudly, and Mrs. McCoy, the music teacher, started banging away on the piano. Casey's teacher, Mr. Floyd, took her elbow and gently led her off the stage. Brenda smirked and mouthed the word *chicken*.

Casey swore she'd never pick up a yo-yo again.

She listened to the *whoooosh* of her breathing in the dark room, counting her breaths the way some people count sheep. But sleep was hiding in the closet with her yo-yo, and it wouldn't come out.

Casey got up and looked out her window.

The yo-yo sign on Mrs. Lombardi's front lawn stared back at her. *YO-YO CONTEST. First Prize $1500.00.* She could still read the letters in the dark.

Not in a million years, Casey whispered.

Not in a million years.

CHAPTER 6

Wednesday morning, the librarian took Casey and Mickey to the section about witches, sorcerers and magic. She handed them three books and went back to her desk. Mickey and Casey took the books to the table and started to read.

"Look!" Mickey gasped. He pointed at a picture of a wand and a recipe for a witches' spell.

Casey read it in a whisper. From time to time the librarian looked up from her work and gave them a curious glance.

"This is a good-luck spell," Casey said. "Is there anything here about learning to read minds?"

"Not that I can see," Mickey said.

"And here's one about curing a bad cough."

"This lady looks a little like Mrs. Lombardi," Casey muttered. She pointed at a little white-haired woman with black eyes.

"It says," read Mickey, "that sometimes you can cure stage fright with a spell."

Casey ignored him and pointed at a picture of a man holding a forked twig. "This man is finding water with a stick," she said.

"You children need any help?" The librarian had come over to their corner to put a book back on the shelf.

Mickey and Casey both jumped. "No!" they said together. Reading about magic and spells was nerve-racking!

The yo-yo sign was flashing brightly as they walked up the road. The neon yo-yo zipped up and down each time the sign lit up and went out. The sign was surrounded by a gang of neighborhood children.

"Wow!" Sammy Brady said. "Fifteen

hundred dollars. That's more money than I can make in two years washing cars!"

"Let me see," said Brenda Bristowe. "I would have to babysit for 214 hours to earn that much money."

"I could get a dirt bike for five hundred," said Sylvia Jarkowski.

I could buy Lightning for that money, thought Casey.

"Did you see that?" Mickey murmured.

"See what?" Casey asked

"See what they've all got in their hands?"

Casey looked. "Yo-yos!" she gasped.

"That's right, Casey Little," Brenda Bristowe said. She turned around and zipped her Fireball Flasher in Casey's face. The yo-yo wobbled and hesitated, but Brenda zapped it back into her hand.

"Those yo-yos practically do their own tricks," Mickey muttered.

Brenda pretended not to hear and smiled a satisfied little smile. "I'm going to win that money, Chicken Little. You're too scared to even try."

All the kids turned and stared.

Casey's face burned bright red, just like Brenda's Fireball.

She turned on her heel and walked toward her house.

Mom was waiting. She had been looking out the window at the crowd of children. Had she heard what Brenda had said?

She didn't say anything. Casey changed into her riding clothes. It was time for her lesson with Lightning. Mom had said she could go one extra time this week since he was going to Geronimo's farm on the weekend. Casey sighed and tried not to look at all the yo-yoing kids on the sidewalk in front of Mrs. Lombardi's.

Lightning trotted over to nudge her pocket the minute she got to the farm. Mom went off to the house to call for Zelda, and Casey fed her last apple to Lightning. She put her cheek on Lightning's neck and listened to him crunch, chew, swallow; crunch, chew, swallow. His neck was warm from the sun, and his mane smelled like hay. Casey closed her eyes.

"Heard that old Lightning's moving on." Casey stopped listening to the inside-horse noises from Lightning's neck and tuned in to the voices that were coming from the barn.

"Yep," Sam, Zelda's hired man said. "It sure is a shame."

"What do you mean?" asked another voice.

"Well, Geronimo's nice enough, but I heard he's buying old Lightning for his daughter."

"Hmmm," said the second voice.

"You see what I mean, then?" said Sam.

Casey pressed her ear against the crack in the barn wall. Mean? What was he talking about?

"You talking about that Deirdre girl?"

"The very one."

"Poor Lightning."

"Yep."

Casey whirled around as a big black car appeared at the end of the driveway. It rumbled along the rutted dirt track, kicking up clouds of dust. The car glided to a stop in front of the paddock and Geronimo's long, spidery legs emerged from the driver's seat. The passenger door opened and a shining brown boot stepped out. It was followed by the skinniest, pointiest girl Casey had ever seen. She took one look at Lightning and sniffed.

"Is that the horse you were talking about, Dad?"

"Sure is. Isn't he a beauty?"

"He's *brown!*"

"Why sure, honey. I told you that."

"I wanted a palomino."

"Now, Deirdre. Lightning here's a very good horse. Gentle and well-schooled. You'd best stick with him."

"I *don't* want a brown horse!"

"Now, Deirdre. How about you take him for a ride first?"

"He looks like he'd come in last in a race of turtles," Deirdre grumbled.

"Now, honey. Let's get him saddled up."

"You do it!" Deirdre turned her back, stalked over to Zelda's front porch and sat down. She looked like she'd just drunk a glass of unsweetened lemonade.

Casey stared. This girl didn't even want Lightning! How could life be so unfair?

Geronimo whistled, and Lightning trotted over to the gate. He swished his tail and pricked his ears forward, looking for treats. Geronimo rubbed the horse's neck and grabbed the halter. Then he led him into the barn.

The girl on the front steps picked up a stone and threw it after her father. It bounced off the barn door and skidded across the dirt until it landed at Casey's feet.

"Hey!" Casey yelled. "You might have hit Lightning with that rock!"

"Mind your own business," snapped the girl. "I can do what I like with my horse!"

"He's not yours until Sunday!" Casey said. She didn't know if that was actually true, but she hoped it was.

"Who're you anyway?" asked the girl. "Some loser who just rides horses but doesn't actually own one?"

"That's the best horse in the world!" Casey said. "Just don't ever forget that!"

"Oh, I get it," the girl muttered. "You're that kid who was saving up to buy old Brownie, there. My dad told me all about it. Told me how hard you'd worked, like it was something special." Her stare chilled Casey to the bone. "He didn't say you were such a loser, though!"

Casey was about to answer when Zelda opened the door and came out on the porch. She said something to Deirdre, then crossed the driveway toward Casey. She struggled with her crutches and sank onto a bale of hay when she got to where Casey was standing.

"Deirdre and her dad want to ride Lightning today, Casey. I'm sorry, but I'm going to have to postpone your lesson. I've talked to your mom. You can come tomorrow, and she said she can bring you back again on Friday to say good-bye. I didn't know Geronimo was coming by or I would have phoned. But Deirdre doesn't have very long to get to know Lightning before she leaves for Montreal."

"Montreal?" Casey asked. "Doesn't she live here with Geronimo?"

"Only some of the time," Zelda answered. "The rest of the time she lives in Montreal with her mother."

"Oh," Casey said.

"Geronimo's going to keep Lightning here on his farm unless Deirdre decides to move him to Montreal."

"What?" Casey turned and looked Zelda in the eyes.

Zelda's kindly face was grave. "I wanted to let you know that Lightning might be moving, Casey," she said. She reached over and patted Casey's arm. "I know this seems hard."

Hard! Casey couldn't even speak. Her sadness was like a great big furball that was caught in her throat. Her eyes burned. She stood up and ran toward the house.

Her mom was waiting in the car. She gave Casey a hug as she climbed into

the front seat. As they drove away, Casey watched over her shoulder as Geronimo led Lightning back into the paddock. Lightning sniffed the air as Deirdre strode over to him. He looked around, as if he was searching for Casey. He nickered and tossed his head.

Deirdre stared after the car, her eyes narrowed. Then she turned to Lightning, stamped her foot and grabbed the reins.

The last thing Casey saw as her mother turned out of the driveway and onto the road was Deirdre's stiff, skinny, hard-edged elbows flailing away at the air, and the glint of a spur as she dug her boots into Lightning's flanks.

 **CHAPTER 7**

Casey marched into her room and threw herself on the bed. Things were getting worse and worse. First Geronimo buys Lightning. Then awful Deirdre shows up. Then Zelda tells her that Lightning might be taken away.

Helpless! That's what she was. Helpless!

Casey propped her cheek on her elbow and stared out her window. The crowd of children in front of Mrs. Lombardi's sign got bigger every day. And every day more things got delivered to her backyard. In addition to the striped tent, the pinball machine and the cotton-candy machine, now there was a trampoline, a dunking machine and a small merry-go-round. Every kid in town hung out in front of the house, sitting on the sidewalk, skateboarding noisily up and down the street, sitting in the trees, hanging off the fences, BMXing off and on the curb, and, worst of all, practicing their yo-yo tricks on Mrs. Lombardi's front lawn. Cars with out-of-province license plates cruised by, and news trucks from as far away as Toronto and Detroit had parked on the street. Casey watched the reporters and cameramen knock on Mrs. Lombardi's door, looking for information. Mrs. Lombardi always offered the reporters cotton candy, but never agreed to do an interview.

Every so often Mrs. Lombardi strolled down her front walk and passed out free cookies to everyone on her property. Trucks came and went, bringing tables, chairs, bags of ice and a loudspeaker system. Two days. The carnival was in two days.

Mickey spotted Casey's face in her window. He darted across the street, charged through her front door and thundered up her stairs. "Hey, Casey," he shouted as he burst into her room, "there's a yo-yo champ here all the way from Michigan!"

Casey sniffed.

"And there's a stage set up at the very back of the tent. Mrs. Lombardi's going to start the competition on Saturday at three o'clock." Mickey took a deep breath and added, "I think you could win it, Casey."

"Can't," Casey said.

Mickey nodded in sympathy. He had been in the front row the day Casey froze.

"If only there was some way you could get rid of that stage fright," he said. "Like a spell or something."

Casey and Mickey stared at each other.

"The book," they said together.

Casey turned and picked up the book

63

that she'd checked out of the library: the book of spells.

A breeze floated through Casey's open window and ruffled the pages. And there, as if by magic, was a special spell.

"*To rid the sufferer of stage fright,*" Casey read. Her voice trembled.

"Wow!" Mickey breathed. "It was like an invisible hand turned the pages to what we were looking for."

"Stop it, Mickey," Casey said. "It was just the wind."

"You sure?" Mickey asked. "How come it flipped right to this page?"

Casey didn't answer. She didn't know.

"What's it say?" Mickey asked.

"*To rid the sufferer of stage fright,*" Casey read again. She continued, "*take three feathers, a pinch of birdseed and a piece of shell from a robin's egg.*" She glanced at Mickey. His eyes were open wide.

"What else?" he said.

"*Dig a hole underneath a black walnut tree. At the stroke of midnight, put the feathers, the birdseed and the shell in the hole and bury them. Then say these magic words: By the light of the moon, I summon the courage of the new day. So that I might fly like the birds when the dawn is new.*"

"Wow!" Mickey said again. "Do you think it would work?"

"Nah," Casey said. She put the book down. Her fingers were shaking. "Probably not."

A great loud cheer rose up from the crowd of children outside Mrs. Lombardi's stone house. Casey and Mickey peered out the window. Brenda Bristowe was looping the loop with her yo-yo.

"Look," said Mickey. "She's doing a triple 'round the world.'"

Casey looked. When she was in her prime, she'd been able to go "round the world" six times.

Up and down the street, kids were yo-yoing. One boy "walked the dog." Another was creating the "Eiffel Tower." Several were sending their yo-yos "round the world."

Yo-yos flashed in all directions. All colors, shapes and sizes. They whizzed, whirred, spun and hummed. The yo-yo sign flashed its neon colors.

On, off. On, off.

Casey thought of Lightning, sniffing the air. She remembered the sweet apple smell of his breath when he neighed a greeting and how he always trotted to the fence when she arrived for her lesson. Then she saw the flash of silver spur as bony Deirdre dug her heels into his glossy brown coat.

"What's that?" she asked.

"What?" Mickey said. He was busy watching the yo-yo antics across the street.

"I heard a thumping."

"Don't hear anything," Mickey answered. He pointed. "That kid just 'split the atom,'" he said excitedly.

"Not possible," Casey said. "That's one of the hardest yo-yo tricks ever invented."

"Look!"

Sure enough, a big kid who looked twelve or thirteen was balancing his yo-yo on the string as it zipped around and around, vibrating like an atom.

Something thumped behind her. Casey looked back over her shoulder.

Mickey didn't seem to notice.

The pages of the book fluttered in the breeze. The silver spurs glinted in the back of Casey's mind.

"Mickey," she said.

"Yeah?" He was hanging out the window, craning his neck to get a better look at the boy who was now the center of attention.

"Meet me tonight."

"Sure," Mickey said. "Where?"

"Behind the Striker house," Casey said. "Under the black walnut tree."

Mickey turned and his eyes went round as Frisbees.

"You mean..." he stammered out.

"Yes," Casey said.

Mickey gulped.

"And bring your feathers."

Mickey nodded.

"Where are you going to find the shell from a robin's egg?" he asked.

Casey went over to her bookshelf and pulled down a bird's nest. "Remember when I found this last spring?"

Mickey looked into the nest of brown twigs. A few sky blue shells, their edges jagged and pale white, lay nestled in the straw.

Casey smiled. "So all we need is bird-seed."

"I'll get some from my canary," said Mickey.

"Good," Casey said.

"You think it will work?" asked Mickey. "It's not exactly scientific."

"I don't know," Casey said. "But it's worth a try."

Mickey's mother came on the porch and hollered, "Mick-eeeeee! Time for dinner." Casey followed Mickey back downstairs.

"Tonight," Casey whispered as Mickey opened the front door.

They made their top-secret handshake.

"Midnight," said Mickey.

"Behind the Striker place," Casey mumbled.

"Go wash your hands, Casey," shouted Mom from the kitchen. "Dad will be home soon. Dinner's ready."

"Okay, Mom," Casey called.

She climbed the stairs and headed for the bathroom. As she passed her bedroom door, she heard it again. A thump. She stopped and listened. Something in her closet was thumping. She was sure of it. She took a deep, wavery breath and crossed the room. She pressed her ear against the closet door and listened.

Thump! Rattle! THUMP!

Casey jumped back.

The closet was silent. She stepped forward and opened the closet door a crack.

Nothing.

She opened the door all the way. Everything was the same. Nothing was moving.

How silly of her.

It wasn't until she was washing her hands that she remembered.

The pile of clothes that she'd buried her yo-yo beneath was on the other side of the closet from where it had been the other night. Not in the very back, on the left, beside her tennis racquet, where it was before, but on the right, leaning up against her baseball bat, just inside the closet door.

Casey gulped, backed away and sat on the side of the bathtub. Impossible! Things didn't move by themselves. She must have been mistaken.

She went back to her room and opened the closet door again. No, the clothes were definitely in a different place. Maybe Mom had been cleaning in her closet—but why would she have left her clothes in a dirty pile? I'll go ask Mom, Casey decided. She reached the bottom of the stairs just as Dad opened the front door. The sound of music drifted in behind him.

"That woman's nuts!" he said as he dropped his briefcase on the floor and headed into the kitchen. "There are cars backed up to Main Street."

Casey went out onto the front porch and stared.

More people were streaming onto her street. Someone had set up a stand selling balloons, and the smell of hot dogs mingled with the exhaust fumes. Brenda Bristowe's father was grilling wieners on the front lawn. Brenda was yo-yoing with two hands. Dogs barked, and Benny stood with his paws against the fence, his tail wagging frantically at everyone who passed. Children rollerbladed by; moms sauntered past, pushing strollers.

Casey was never going to be able to perform her yo-yo tricks in front of a crowd like this!

Magic or no magic. Not in a million years.

Mrs. Lombardi waved from her chair across the street.

Reluctantly, Casey waved back.

"Casey," yelled Mom, "dinnertime!"

Casey turned to go.

But not before Mrs. Lombardi gave her a great big just-between-you-and-me secret wink!

 **CHAPTER 8**

A watery moon cast a pale light on the ground, causing the shadows of the bushes to dance like ghosts across the grass. Casey's teeth chattered as she and Mickey crept across her backyard and through the overgrown hedge that surrounded the Striker property. The giant black walnut tree loomed up in the back of the yard. The houses were dark. Mickey's flashlight threw a tunnel of light on the uneven ground.

"Are you sure this is a good idea?" Mickey asked.

"Shhhh," Casey commanded. She clutched the bag of feathers and shells

in her right hand. In her left, she dragged a spade she'd taken from her father's toolshed.

An owl hooted softly from somewhere overhead. A bush rustled off to the side, and a cat howled in the distance. Two shiny eyes glared at them from the Frasers' garden.

"Raccoons," breathed Mickey. His voice shook as he spoke.

"Hurry up," Casey whispered. She plunged her hand into her pocket, clutched her lucky horseshoe and rubbed the edge for courage. It was much scarier out in the dark than she had thought it would be. It had seemed like such a simple idea at the time. Dig a hole, chant a few words and bury the spell ingredients under a tree at midnight. What could be easier?

"Sure is dark out here," Mickey said. His teeth chattered.

Casey put down her bag. "Shine the light here," she commanded. She pointed at a spot directly under the big old tree. Spiky walnut pods had formed on its ancient branches. It seemed to be watching. Casey wondered if it was amused by what it saw.

She stuck the pointed end of the spade into the dirt and pushed down with her foot. She had to work hard, but in ten minutes she had dug a hole the size of a bucket.

Casey took a deep breath and opened the bag of spell ingredients. First she lined the hole with two feathers. Then she sprinkled the canary seed on top of them. Finally she removed the robin's eggshells from inside a cotton-lined box.

"What do we do now?" Mickey asked.

"We wait until exactly midnight, then say the chant," Casey said. "I memorized it."

Mickey pressed the button on his wristwatch and an eerie green glow lit up his face. "Countdown," he said. "Get ready. Ten, nine, eight, seven, six, five, four, three," he glanced at Casey. She was kneeling with her eyes squeezed shut. "Two," he continued. "ONE!"

She clenched her fists under her chin and chanted in a clear, steady voice: "By the light of the moon, I summon the courage of the new day. So that I might fly like the birds when the dawn is new."

A sudden breeze ruffled Casey's hair. Then a deathly quiet fell on the yard. All the night sounds stopped. The caterwauling. The rustling of small critters through the grass. The creaking of the old tree.

"Sure is quiet," Mickey whispered into the complete silence.

"Sure is," Casey agreed.

"Uh, I'd like to go now," Mickey said. His voice shook.

"Me too," Casey said. "First I have to fill up the hole."

"I'll help." Mickey dropped his flashlight and fell on his knees. He started shoving handfuls of dirt into the hole. The spell ingredients disappeared. The smell of the freshly dug earth rose up into Casey's nostrils. It smelled like autumn and compost and dead leaves.

"Let's scram," Mickey said. He jumped up and brushed the dirt off his knees. "It's creepy out here."

Together they doubled back across the yard. The night sounds had started again. All the living creatures exhaled, drew breath, exhaled again.

In Casey's backyard, Mickey flicked off his flashlight. The back porch lamp cast a yellow pool of light across the grass.

Casey and Mickey did their secret handshake. "Feel any different?" Mickey asked.

Casey thought about it. "No. Not really," she answered.

"It probably takes time to work," Mickey said.

"Maybe." Casey looked at her arms. Her hands. Her fingers. They felt the same. She listened to her heart beating. She imagined standing in front of fifty children with a yo-yo in her hand. Her fingers clenched and her heart raced.

Mickey watched her with a hopeful look on his face.

"Let's sleep on it," Casey said. She flexed her fingers and breathed deeply.

Mickey nodded. "See you tomorrow," he said, then dashed off to his house.

Casey let herself in the back door and crept up the stairs to her room. She put the spade in her closet. She would return it to the toolshed tomorrow.

She stared at the pile of clothes in the right-hand corner of the closet floor. She squinted. Her yo-yo was under those clothes. She could feel it looking at her.

She shut the door firmly and went to the window. She stared at Mrs. Lombardi's house. The backyard where the striped tent was seemed to glow in the dark. Tomorrow, it seemed to say.

Tomorrow, she decided, she would try one trick.

Just one.

She closed her eyes and thought about the magic spell. Would it work?

She opened her eyes and stared at Mrs. Lombardi's window. She thought she saw something. Yes. She was sure she could see the silhouette of Mrs. Lombardi standing in her front window, giving her a thumbs-up.

 **CHAPTER 9**

Casey woke to the sounds of birdsong. She breathed deeply. It was Thursday. She glanced at her closet. Slowly, she raised her fingers to her face and cracked a knuckle. No time like the present, she thought. Would the spell work?

She jumped out of bed, trotted across her room and flung open the closet door. Without hesitating she kicked aside the pile of old clothes. They smelled like suntan lotion and seaweed, and Casey remembered wearing them to the beach last June, right before she'd frozen solid in front of the whole school.

She picked up the yo-yo. It didn't seem so scary now that she was holding it in her hand. She looped the string over her finger and palmed the red shiny surface. Then she let it drop. The yo-yo descended the string and zipped right back up into her palm.

That wasn't so hard, Casey decided. She practiced a couple more times. Each time she felt more confident. Now, she thought, it was time to try something harder. She "walked the dog," sent the yo-yo "round the world" and even "rocked the cradle." The tricks came back to her with ease. The spell seemed to be working!

"Casey!" Mom shouted. "Mickey's here!"

Mickey clattered up the stairs. He stood in her bedroom door and pointed at the yo-yo in her hand. "Did it work?"

Casey looped the loop.

Mickey whooped.

"You're going to win for sure!" he said.

Outside, the crowds of children had continued to gather. Tomorrow was opening day at Mrs. Lombardi's carnival.

"Let's go see what's happening," Mickey said.

"Not until you've eaten some breakfast," Mom said from the doorway. She saw the yo-yo in Casey's hand, but she didn't say anything.

After breakfast, Mickey and Casey crossed the street. Mrs. Lombardi was in her front yard, handing out free donuts. She waved them over.

"Hi, kids," she said. She flashed her dimples, then looked a little longer at Casey. "Tomorrow's the big day!" Then she hurried away to give a donut to a toddler from down the block.

Casey gulped. Brenda came down her walk and sidled up to Casey. "Cluck, cluck," she whispered in Casey's ear. Casey jumped.

"Stop it, Brenda," Mickey said.

"I know who bought your horse, Casey," Brenda continued, sticking her tongue out at Mickey.

"What do you mean?" asked Casey.

"I know Deirdre Patchett from horse

shows. She's so cool! And my dad says Mr. Patchett is one of the richest men in the whole county! My dad worked with him a long time ago."

"So what?" Mickey challenged. "Money isn't everything."

"Hah!" Brenda said. "It is if you want a horse. Right, Casey?" Brenda smirked and walked away, clucking.

"Don't mind her," Mickey said.

But Casey had already gone.

Up in her room she stared at her yo-yo. If she really, really practiced, maybe she could do it. Maybe she could win that money. She couldn't let Lightning go to Deirdre. She had to win! She practiced all morning, only taking a break to make her pet-sitting rounds. She went to all the jobs on her side of the street through the backyards so she wouldn't have to run into Brenda. She didn't even want to see Mickey.

"Casey!" hollered Mom. "It's time to go to the stable!"

"Can't!" Casey answered.

"Are you all right?" Mom asked.

"Sure," Casey lied. "I just don't feel like riding today."

"Tomorrow's going to be your last chance!" Mom said, coming up the stairs. "Are you sure you want to miss today?"

Casey stuffed her yo-yo under her pillow. She wasn't going to think about that. She couldn't.

Mom came to the door of her room. "Are you positive you don't want to go?"

Casey nodded. Mom scanned the room as if she was looking for something. Casey sat on her bed, her heart thumping.

"All right, then," Mom said. "If that's what you want. I'll call Zelda."

When Mom left, Casey fished her yo-yo out from under her pillow. It seemed to vibrate in her hand as if charged by an electric current. Casey jumped and dropped it onto the floor, where it glowed like a ruby that had been hit with fire. Casey leaned forward and picked it up. Her hand felt strong. She might just have a chance to win the contest after all.

She peeked out her window. Brenda Bristowe ran down her walk and climbed into her car. She was wearing her riding clothes! She called to Casey as her mom backed down the driveway, "I phoned Deirdre and asked her to go riding with me today! We're going to take Lightning out on the trail!" Then the car drove away.

Casey's heart cracked. She hoped Deirdre would be gentle with her horse. Then she went back to practicing her yo-yo tricks. She was going to win, she decided. No matter what! Lightning was depending on her.

 **CHAPTER 10**

Friday morning, Casey and Mickey went over to Mrs. Lombardi's right after breakfast.

"Want to help?" asked Mrs. Lombardi when she saw them.

"Sure!" Mickey said.

"Good boy," Mrs. Lombardi said. She pointed at the sno-cone machine. "I need someone sensible to operate the controls. Mickey, I think you're just the person to do it."

Mickey galloped off. "Now, Casey," Mrs. Lombardi said. "How would you like to sign people up for the yo-yo contest? It's tomorrow afternoon, you know."

Casey nodded. She knew. She definitely knew.

Mrs. Lombardi walked her over to a table and chairs. A long line of people waited to put their names down.

"Why don't you start with your own name?" Mrs. Lombardi asked. She raised her eyebrows, and her white, wispy hair seemed to blow away from her head like tendrils of smoke.

"I'm not sure."

"Really?" Mrs. Lombardi raised her eyebrows even higher.

Casey sat down. Mrs. Lombardi patted her shoulder and trotted off to the pinball machine. "Well, think about it," she called over her shoulder.

All morning, Casey wrote down the names of the yo-yo hopefuls. Two hundred and fifty names later, her fingers were cramped and sore from writing. Mickey waved at her from the sno-cone machine. Casey stared at her list. She sighed, took a deep breath and wrote *Casey Little*.

Mickey whooped, and Mrs. Lombardi appeared from nowhere. "Good girl," she said. "Good girl."

Casey put down her pen and shook out her arms. She headed for home, grabbed her yo-yo and let Benny out in his yard. All afternoon, Benny kept her company while she practiced. The happy shrieks of the children, the noise of the pinball machine and the smells of the cotton candy didn't distract her once. She gulped her food at dinner, and for once her mother didn't say anything. After dinner, she went back to Benny's and practiced and practiced until her fingers were numb. The sounds of the carnival didn't pull her away from Benny's backyard. Benny watched her with solemn eyes. He thumped his tail every time she completed a trick. After it got dark, Casey went to her room and practiced some more. Casey pushed herself harder and harder. By midnight, the carnival music and lights had shut down. Mom came to the door and told Casey it was time for bed.

"Don't be disappointed tomorrow if you don't win," Mom said when she tucked Casey in.

"I've got to win," Casey whispered. "For Lightning."

"I know," said Mom. She smoothed Casey's hair.

Casey couldn't sleep. She replayed her yo-yo moves over and over in her mind. At one o'clock she decided to put her lucky horseshoe under her pillow for good luck. But when she stuck her hand in the pocket of her jeans, it wasn't there.

Casey's breath jammed in her throat. Not there! She'd had it when she and Mickey had placed the spell; she'd rubbed it for luck. She must have dropped it when she was digging the hole. Casey shut her eyes and forced herself to remember exactly what had happened. She'd dug the hole and then...Oh NO! She must have pulled it out when she'd pulled out an extra feather she'd stuffed in her jeans' pocket. Would she be able to find it before the yo-yo competition?

In the morning, Casey shot out of the house before her parents had cracked an eyelid. She dashed through the dew-damp grass and ran for the freshly dug earth under the black walnut tree. As she got closer, she dropped to her knees and felt her way along the grass. Nothing! The grass just squished under her fingers and wet the knees of her jeans. Casey flopped down on her stomach and lay her head in the wet grass. How could she have been so careless? Her grandmother had given her that miniature horseshoe when she was five years old. It was her lucky charm. She'd never, never, never win the yo-yo contest without it!

The birds watched her suspiciously as she lay there. Somewhere a phone rang, a door slammed and the smell of coffee wafted to her on the breeze. Casey dragged herself to her feet. She had to get back or her parents would worry. And she didn't want to explain where she'd been, because then she'd have to explain about sneaking out at midnight to cast a magic anti-stage-fright spell. Somehow, she just didn't think her parents would understand.

Casey forced herself to go home. She forced herself up the stairs to her room. She forced herself to pick up her yo-yo and practice. She wouldn't tell anyone about losing her lucky horseshoe. Not even Mickey.

Mickey came by right after breakfast.

Brenda Bristowe was on his heels.

"That's Deirdre Patchett!" said Brenda. Casey looked over Brenda's shoulder. She saw the long black car with the yo-yo dangling from the rearview mirror. She could see Deirdre's spiky hair and pointed nose in the front seat.

"What are they doing here?" Casey asked.

Mickey shrugged his shoulders. "Probably came to see the yo-yo competition like everybody else," he said.

Casey wasn't sure. She was positive Deirdre looked at Brenda and smiled as she drove by.

"Sure are a lot of people here," said Mickey. He pointed at the news trucks that were lined up along the street. Casey's face flushed. She gulped. This wasn't anything like the school yo-yo competition.

This was a thousand times worse.

Every seat was filled. As Mom, Dad, Mickey and Casey crossed the street, Casey's heart galloped around her chest the way Lightning galloped around the paddock.

The first contestant did three simple tricks. The crowd applauded politely.

Casey took her place in the lineup. A girl in front of her yo-yoed steadily without looking right or left. The boy from Michigan "split the atom," but the yo-yo wobbled on the last rotation. The crowd was laughing, pointing and talking. Brenda's turn came and went. She did an excellent "walk the dog," "round the world" and "Eiffel Tower." She smirked at Casey as she came off the stage. Casey's palms were slick with sweat. As she got closer to the stage, her throat dried up and her neck muscles tightened. Three people were left in front of her. Casey tried to remember the words of the magic spell. "So I can fly like a bird when the dawn is new."

Mrs. Lombardi appeared at her side. "Almost there, Casey," she said.

The girl on the stage was working with two yo-yos, sending them rocketing in two directions at once.

"Well, that's impressive," Mrs. Lombardi said.

Casey nodded. She would never win this competition. She could kiss the money and Lightning good-bye.

"Casey Little!" cried Mr. Bristowe, who was acting as master of ceremonies.

"Good luck, dear," said Mrs. Lombardi. Her eyes twinkled.

Casey's knees knocked together as she climbed the steps to the little stage. The faces of the crowd blurred in front of her as she turned to face the audience. She blinked, and her vision cleared.

Mickey had so many limbs crossed that he looked like a pretzel. He was staring at Casey with his eyes crossed, his legs crossed, his arms crossed, his fingers crossed and his hands crossed. Casey smiled, and some of the tension lifted off her neck. She rolled her shoulders, flexed her fingers, took a deep breath, muttered "So I can fly like a bird when the dawn is new" one more time and let fly.

Once again the yo-yo vibrated mysteriously in her hand. It slept, it spun, it hummed and squealed. It responded to the lightest touch and lifted smoothly into Casey's fingers. Casey performed her three hardest tricks. The crowd hushed, the sun emerged from behind a cloud and tears blinded Casey's eyes. When she finished her final trick, the crowd went wild, stamping their feet, whistling and applauding. Casey bowed and walked to the side of the stage where Mickey had uncrossed himself and was jumping up and down like a Mexican jumping bean.

"You did it!" he shouted. "You did it!"

Casey couldn't stop smiling. She had conquered her fear. The yo-yo was her friend. The crowd was her friend. First Mom, then Dad, then Mrs. Lombardi gave her a giant hug.

"The judges have made their decision," called Mr. Bristowe. All the contestants took their seats. A judge passed a piece of paper from the judges' stand along the line of spectators in front of the stage. Only then did Casey notice something odd.

A judge she hadn't noticed before was sitting in the front row: Deirdre Patchett.

"What's she doing there?" Casey asked Mickey.

Mickey shrugged. "I heard Mr. Bristowe tell Brenda that Deirdre's dad owns a yo-yo company, and he's donating the prize money!"

So that's what Brenda and Deirdre's secret smile had meant! Casey sat down with a *whump!* right on the ground. She didn't like the sound of that news one bit. A shiver ran up her spine, and she looked around.

Deirdre's eyes were on her. They were boring right through her, like twin laser beams.

On stage, Mr. Bristowe handed the envelope to Mrs. Lombardi. She smiled, tore it open and read the name of the winner. Her eyes scanned the crowd, bounced off Brenda Bristowe, skimmed over the boy from Michigan and came to rest on Casey.

Then she said, "First place in the first annual Harmony Beach Yo-Yo Competition, and one thousand, five hundred dollars in prize money, goes to Ralph Larrabee from Flint, Michigan."

Casey gulped. Mickey squatted beside her and said, "No way. Casey, you were way better."

"Second prize, and five hundred dollars, goes to Brenda Bristowe."

The crowd muttered a little. Brenda flounced up onto the stage and took the check from her father's hand. "Congratulations, honey," Mr. Bristowe said. He beamed out over the audience.

"No way!" Mickey shouted.

"Shhh!" Casey said.

"And third prize, a brand-new, extra-special, super-charged, limited-edition Patchett yo-yo, goes to...Casey Little."

The crowd applauded politely. Casey made her way up to the stage.

Mr. Bristowe handed her a yo-yo. Casey smiled and said thank-you.

"No way!" Mickey chanted from the crowd.

Mrs. Lombardi put her arm around Mickey's shoulders. "Hush now, Mickey," she said. "Sometimes it is hard to understand why things happen the way they do."

When Casey came down the steps, her mother was waiting. "Sorry, hon," she said. Her face was sad.

Casey was not going to cry. She tore away from her mom and walked over to the Richardsons' backyard. She sat and hugged Benny and stared at the sky. She'd done her best. So what if the darn old spell hadn't worked?

"It worked," Mrs. Lombardi said. Casey looked up. Mrs. Lombardi had followed her. But how had she known what Casey was thinking? How had she known about the spell?

"What do you mean, it worked?" Casey demanded. "I lost."

"I think the spell was meant to cure your stage fright," Mrs. Lombardi said. "It certainly did that!"

"But I lost Lightning!" Casey moaned.

"That may be true, Casey," Mrs. Lombardi answered. "Who can say?"

Benny licked Casey's face. Mom appeared at the fence. "Are you all right, Casey?" she asked.

"Mom," Casey said, "will you take me out to Zelda's? I want to say good-bye to Lightning. I want to explain." Casey sniffed. She had to tell Lightning that she'd tried. Even if she'd failed. It was important that he know she loved him before Deirdre had a chance to take him away.

"Sure," said Mom.

"Right now," Casey said.

Mom looked surprised. "Can't it wait until tomorrow?"

"No," said Casey. "He may be gone tomorrow! I have to see him today."

Mrs. Lombardi smiled; her dimples sank into her cheeks.

"Come on then," said Mom. "Let's go."

As they backed out of the driveway, Casey had one final look at the carnival. It was all over. Only a few stragglers were left. The music was silent. Only then did Casey remember that she had forgotten to ask Mrs. Lombardi how she'd known about the spell.

Only one car was left in front of the house, Geronimo's big shiny limousine. And leaning against the door was Deirdre.

Casey felt Deirdre watching as she and Mom drove away. She even felt those eyes on the back of her head after the car had turned the corner and left Willow Street far behind.

# CHAPTER 11

Lightning nudged Casey's pocket. Casey pulled out the apple she'd brought from home, and Lightning munched it happily.

"I'm sorry I can't buy you," Casey whispered into his ear. He twitched both ears back and forth as if he understood everything she was saying. "I tried, Lightning," Casey said. Her voice caught and she cleared her throat. "I really tried." Lightning rubbed the side of his face up and down against Casey's arm.

Zelda and Mom watched from the porch. From time to time, Zelda leaned over and said something to Mom, but Casey couldn't hear what was said. She climbed up on the fence and lay her face on Lightning's glossy neck. He hooked his chin over the top slat and stayed perfectly still. He knows, Casey thought. He knows this might be the last time I get to see him.

The sun had cooled in the sky. Casey shivered. Lightning swished his tail and nickered. Casey looked over her shoulder. A cloud of dust rose from the dirt road that led to Zelda's farm. And as the cloud of dust cleared, Casey could see what was coming.

It was a long, black limousine.

Geronimo's car.

It glided to a stop in front of Zelda's porch. Mom and Zelda stopped talking. Lightning pawed the ground. The car door opened, and Deirdre unfolded herself and stepped out. Geronimo appeared from the driver's side.

Deirdre took one look at Casey and stalked over to the fence.

"What are you doing here?" she demanded.

Lightning pawed the ground.

Deirdre glared at the horse. He flattened his ears.

"I asked you a question," Deirdre said. She stared at Casey.

"I came to say good-bye to Lightning," Casey said. She put her arm around Lightning's neck. Deirdre sneered.

"I'm taking that horse to Montreal," she said. Her black eyes glinted in the sun.

"Why?" Casey asked. "Don't you want a horse here when you come to visit your dad?"

"I'm going to get him to buy me another one," Deirdre said. She smiled: a thin-lipped smile that wasn't really a smile at all. "He does anything I tell him to."

"Why can't you get another horse in Montreal and leave Lightning here?" Casey asked. Lightning nodded his head up and down as if he agreed completely.

"I'll let you in on a little secret," Deirdre said. She leaned forward and whispered, "It's because I don't want you around MY horse!" She leaned back and laughed. The sound made Casey think of cymbals crashing together.

"I heard that."

Casey peeked over Lightning's back, and Deirdre whirled around.

Geronimo was standing beside the gate. His basset-hound face drooped.

"Oh, Daddy," Deirdre said in a little girl's voice. "Please don't be mad at me. I..."

Geronimo held up his hand. "I don't think you need to say another word, Deirdre, honey."

Deirdre relaxed. She smiled at her father. "You understand then, Daddy?"

"I understand more than you might think," Geronimo answered. He reached over and patted Lightning's neck. Lightning whinnied. "Good boy," Geronimo said. He looked thoughtful. Then he turned and walked back to the house.

"See what I mean?" Deirdre hissed when Geronimo was out of earshot. "Putty in my hands."

"Casey!" shouted Mom. "Time to go."

Casey gave Lightning one last hug. He raced from one end of the paddock to the other as Casey walked slowly back to the car. Her mom gave her a hug when she climbed in, but Casey couldn't stop the tears. They welled out of her eyes and plopped like huge raindrops on her jeans. Beside her, Mom heaved a sigh.

They drove in silence all the way home.

When they pulled up to the house, Dad was sitting on the front steps waiting for them.

He jumped up in excitement the minute he saw the car.

"Casey!" Dad shouted. He waved.

Mom looked at Casey. "What the heck?" she said.

Dad ran down the walk and yanked open Casey's door. He took one look at her soggy jeans and red eyes and yelled, "Well, no more tears for you, my dear. Zelda just called. You must call her back this instant. I promised to let her give you the news."

Casey sniffed. Dad's smile was as bright as the sun.

"Hurry up! Hurry up!" Dad said. He dragged her up the walk.

Mom followed. She kept saying, "Now, Richard, now, Richard, take it easy."

Inside the house, Dad handed Casey the phone and dialed the number. Then he stepped back and gave Mom a big kiss on the cheek. He couldn't stop beaming.

"Hi, Zelda," Casey said.

Casey listened for two minutes. Then she turned off the phone. Mom and Dad watched, their hands clasped together.

"Well?" Dad said.

"Yeeeeeee-HAAAAAAAW!" Casey shouted.

Mom and Dad danced around the kitchen. The glasses rattled in the cupboards.

"Why is everyone so happy?" Mickey asked, peering through the screen door.

"Geronimo's giving Lightning to ME!" Casey whooped.

"What?" Mickey said. He opened the door

and came in without being asked. They all danced around the kitchen together.

"Why?" Mom asked after she'd collapsed in a chair and fanned herself with a piece of the Saturday paper.

"Because he doesn't think Deirdre deserves him," Dad explained. "Zelda phoned to tell me that as soon as you and Casey drove off, Geronimo came over to her and told her that he thought Miss Deirdre needed to learn the value of things. He decided she wasn't ready to take care of her own horse, so he'd take it kindly if our Miss Casey here," Dad stopped and nodded at Casey, "would consider accepting his offer of Lightning. He even said Casey could keep Lightning on his ranch.

"When I told him we couldn't afford to buy Lightning, he said that was no problem because he'd never seen a Yo-Yo Queen quite like our Casey," and here Dad stopped and took a sip of his coffee.

Mom, Mickey and Casey all punched him in the shoulder.

"Don't stop now!" Mom said.

Dad laughed and continued. "He said that he felt there might have been a mix-up with the results of today's yo-yo contest and that Casey was the rightful winner. So he offered Lightning instead of the prize money. He hoped you wouldn't mind, Casey."

"Mind?" Casey jumped up and down in her seat. "Mind?"

"No," Dad said. "I told him I didn't think you'd mind."

"What about the board?" Casey asked. "I can't afford the board!"

"Well," Dad replied. "Here's something else. He wants Casey here to do some ads for his new super-powered, limited-edition Patchett special. That should more than pay for the board."

Casey couldn't stop laughing. She and Mickey whirled around the kitchen until the ceiling spun and the lights were a blur of yellow and white. They collapsed on the floor and giggled.

"Mrs. Lombardi!" Casey shouted as

soon as she caught her breath. "We have to tell Mrs. Lombardi!"

Mom and Dad smiled as Casey and Mickey dashed out the door.

The little stone house stood silent and calm after all the noise of the carnival.

Casey and Mickey rushed up the walk and banged on the door. The white lace curtains shook with the force of their knocking.

The door stayed shut.

"That's weird," said Mickey. "It doesn't look like she's home."

"Where would she go?" Casey asked. "She was right here a few hours ago. Did she say she was going anywhere?"

"Uh-uh," Mickey said.

"Hey, you kids," yelled someone from the sidewalk. "What are you doing?"

Casey and Mickey peered over the hedge. A short man carrying a tent pole was loading the tent into a rental truck. Other trucks appeared in front of the house, a whole fleet of trucks: a cotton-candy rental truck, a pinball machine rental truck, a sno-cone rental truck and a merry-go-round rental truck.

"Have you seen the lady that lives here?" Casey shouted back.

"Nope." The man pushed the tent pole into the back of the truck. He was fat and bald and wore a cap pushed back on his head. "We just had orders to come and pick all this stuff up at seven o'clock sharp this evening."

A pair of workmen carted the pinball machine down the driveway. Another pair of workers with the cotton-candy machine followed. A few pink wisps of floss stuck to their overalls.

"Have you seen Mrs. Lombardi?" Casey asked a tall skinny man with a droopy mustache.

"Who?"

"The lady who lives here," said Mickey.

"Sorry," the man said. He and his partner got in their truck and drove away.

One by one the workmen packed up their equipment and left. It didn't seem to take any time at all. When they were gone, the house looked as if Mrs. Lombardi, the carnival and the yo-yo contest had never existed.

 # CHAPTER 12

"Good girl, Casey," said the photographer. He snapped six shots, one after the other.

Lightning shifted his weight under her and batted his ears back and forth as if to say he'd had enough of having his picture taken.

"Just one more!" the photographer said, getting down on one knee and angling his camera. "Now, Casey, hold that Patchett Special Lightning-Bolt Yo-yo a little higher, so's we can see the printing real clear. That's it! Now, big smile!"

Casey grinned. Geronimo waved from the barn door, and Mom smiled from a nearby bale of hay. Lightning swished his tail.

The photographer started to put away his camera. "All finished, Casey. You and Lightning are great subjects."

Geronimo strode over. He covered the distance in ten steps with his long, spindly legs. Casey thought of Deirdre and shivered. Geronimo fed Lightning a carrot.

"Mind if I take him for a ride, Mom?" Casey shouted at her mom.

"Just a short one, Casey," her mom answered. "We've got the new neighbor coming for dinner."

"Okay." Casey and Lightning trotted around the ring, let themselves out the gate and headed down the trail. A light breeze fluffed Casey's hair and rippled the grass. Casey began to sing. The long grass dipped and swayed in time as she and Lightning passed.

Back at the barn, Casey cleaned Lightning's bridle and brushed him thoroughly before putting him in his stall.

"I'll see you tomorrow, boy," Casey whispered in his ear. He nodded as if he understood.

At home, Casey set the table for four. Mom bustled about the kitchen, fixing dinner. Casey went out onto the porch. Mickey saw her and came over. He was carrying his detective case.

Together they sat on the steps and stared at the stone house.

"A good detective would be able to figure it out," Mickey said.

"I don't know," Casey answered. She patted Mickey's arm.

"Nope. A person can't just disappear into thin air like that."

"Well," Casey said, "Dad said she must have planned to move out like that all along. All the arrangements to sell the house were made before she left."

"But why did she go?" Mickey said. He turned and faced Casey. He put his hands on his hips. "And why didn't she say good-bye?"

"It's a mystery," Casey agreed.

"What's the new neighbor like, anyway?" Mickey asked.

"I don't know," Casey answered. "I never met her before."

The door of the stone house opened. Casey and Mickey stood up. A young woman was crossing the street. She had a box in one hand and a bag in the other. She was short and plump.

As she got closer, Casey could see that she was wearing a ponytail and that her hair sizzled off her head in all directions. There was something familiar about the way she walked, but Casey couldn't put her finger on exactly what it was. Mickey's breathing slowed.

The lady made her way across the street. She smiled at Casey and Mickey, and dimples poked holes in her cheeks. Her eyes were merry.

"Hello," she said in a cheery voice.

"Hello," Casey said. She couldn't stop staring.

"H-h-h-hello," Mickey stammered.

"You must be Mickey," the lady said.

She handed Mickey the box. "I brought these for you." Mickey reached out and took the box. He had no need to look inside. He knew what it was.

"And you must be Casey," the lady said.

"Yes," Casey said.

"I'm Sybil," the woman said in her happy voice. "And I've got a present for you as well." She handed the bag to Casey.

"Well, tally-ho!" Sybil said and went up the stairs and knocked on the door.

Mom let her in. "Why, Casey," she said. "Why didn't you show Sybil into the house?"

Casey's voice had disappeared. She tried to speak, but couldn't.

"Casey," said Mom.

"Oh, that's all right," Sybil said. "They're just surprised to see me."

Mom looked confused, but she didn't say anything else. She invited Sybil into the house, and the screen door closed with a slap.

Mickey closed his mouth. He opened his box. He was right. Donuts. His favorite, double-chocolate-sprinkled donuts. He raised his eyes to Casey. "How did she know?" he asked.

Casey cleared her throat. "That's really weird, Mickey," she said. "Did Sybil look sort of familiar to you?"

Mickey nodded. "Sort of. But I can't say why..." He stared at the donuts. "Donuts," he said again.

"Me neither. But there's something about her."

"What did she give you?"

"I don't know." Casey opened the bag. It was her lucky horseshoe—the one she'd lost the night she and Mickey had cast the stage-fright spell under the black walnut tree in the Strikers' backyard—the one she'd looked for and hadn't been able to find.

Mickey's eyes widened even further. Casey and Mickey stared at each other.

The front door opened, and Sybil stood on the porch. Her yellow ponytail looked electrified in the afternoon sun. "Dinner's ready," she said.

Mickey picked up his detective kit. Sybil smiled. "Cracked any cases yet, Mickey?" she asked.

Mickey shook his head. "Well, I better go." He ran down the walk. He carried his detective kit in one hand and his box of donuts in the other.

Sybil held the door open for Casey. Casey put her lucky horseshoe in her pocket. She didn't think she'd ask Sybil how she found it.

Sybil watched her stuff her hand in her pocket. When Casey lifted her eyes, she saw Sybil watching her. They stared at each other for a whole minute.

"You know," Casey said, "you remind me a lot of someone. Someone who used to live in your house."

Sybil nodded wisely. "You'll have to tell me all about it," she said.

"She was an old lady. Who kind of knew things," Casey said.

"Knew things?"

"Like our names and our favorite foods. Things like that," Casey finished lamely.

"Hmmmm," Sybil said. She smiled.

"Do you know where she went?" Casey asked.

"Probably went someplace where she was needed," Sybil said.

"Needed?"

"You never know where you're going to be needed in this world," Sybil said. "That's why I'm here."

Casey stood dead still. Sybil's laughter tinkled above her.

"There are still some things to be done here in Harmony Beach," Sybil said in a cheery, let's-roll-up-our-sleeves kind of voice.

"What kind of things?" Casey muttered.

"Well, we'll just have to wait and see, now won't we?" Sybil said. She curled her lips into a mysterious smile. Her dimples punctuated her cheeks. She crossed her hands in front of her, turned and went into the house.

But not before she gave Casey a great big just-between-you-and-me wink!

Nancy Belgue loves yo-yos and magic and in *Casey Little—Yo-Yo Queen* she has found the perfect way to blend them together. Nancy is also the author of *The Scream of the Hawk*, a Silver Birch nominee for 2005, and *Summer on the Run*, both published by Orca. She lives with her family in Kingsville, Ontario.

Orca Young Readers

Daughter of Light	martha attema
Hero	martha attema
Things Are Looking Up, Jack	Dan Bar-el
Casey Little—Yo-Yo Queen	**Nancy Belgue**
Dog Days	Becky Citra
Chance and the Butterfly	Maggie de Vries
Belle of Batoche	Jacqueline Guest
Peggy's Letters	**Jacqueline Halsey**
Dinosaurs on the Beach	Marilyn Helmer
Birdie for Now	Jean Little
Forward, Shakespeare!	**Jean Little**
Rescue Pup	Jean Little
Catching Spring	Sylvia Olsen
Murphy and Mousetrap	Sylvia Olsen
Discovering Emily	Jacqueline Pearce
Emily's Dream	Jacqueline Pearce
The Reunion	Jacqueline Pearce
Jesse's Star	Ellen Schwartz
Any Pet Will Do	Nancy Shouse
Under a Living Sky	**Joseph Simons**
The Keeper and the Crows	Andrea Spalding
Phoebe and the Gypsy	Andrea Spalding
Jo's Triumph	Nikki Tate
Five Stars for Emily	Kathleen Cook Waldron
Just Call Me Joe	Frieda Wishinsky